Help

Written by Jill Eggleton
Illustrated by Paul Könye

Rigby

Little Bird sat on Rhino.

"I am going to stay
with you," she said.
"I can help you."

Rhino looked at Little Bird.

"You can't help me,"
he said.
"You are a little bird.
You cannot stay with me."

Rhino put down his head.

“**Go away!**” he shouted.
Whummmp!

“I’m not going,”
said Little Bird.

Little Bird saw a helicopter.

The helicopter came down
and a man got out.

"Good," said the man.
"A rhino!"

Little Bird went
squawk, squawk, squawk!

Rhino looked up.
He saw the man.

Rhino put down his head.

He ran after the man.

The man got into
the helicopter and
he went away!

“See,” said Little Bird.
“I **can** help you!”

“OK,” said Rhino.
“You can stay with me!”

A Story Sequence

1

2

3

4

Guide Notes

Title: Help for Rhino!
Stage: Early (2) – Yellow

Genre: Fiction
Approach: Guided Reading
Processes: Thinking Critically, Exploring Language, Processing Information
Written and Visual Focus: Story Sequence
Word Count: 124

Thinking Critically

(sample questions)

- What do you think this story could be about?
- Focus on the title and discuss.
- Why do you think Rhino didn't want Little Bird to stay with him in the beginning?
- Why do you think the man in the helicopter wanted to look at Rhino?
- How do you know that Little Bird was a nice bird?
- How do you think Rhino could help Little Bird?

Exploring Language

Terminology

Title, cover, illustrations, author, illustrators

Vocabulary

Interest words: helicopter, whummp, squawk
High-frequency words: stay, with, good
Positional words: into, on, down, out, up

Print Conventions

Capital letter for sentence beginnings and names (**L**ittle **B**ird, **R**hino), periods, commas, quotation marks, exclamation marks